MY Monet ART MUSEUM

On every page there
are empty frames where
the sticker paintings belong.
Read the clues inside the frames
to help you put each sticker
in the right space.

Carole Armstrong

PHILOMEL BOOKS

Painting out of doors

When the French artist Claude Monet was a young man, he would go into the countryside to paint. In those days most artists painted only rough sketches out of doors, then finished their paintings in a studio. Monet was different. To make his pictures look fresh and lively, he would finish them in the open air.

Impression: Sunrise 1872

Monet and other painters were nicknamed "Impressionists," after the title of this painting. The name was meant as an insult, by people who didn't like the way Monet had painted an impression of the harbor, instead of copying exactly what he saw.

Regatta at Argenteuil 1872

Monet often painted the boats on the river at Argenteuil, the village near Paris where he lived. Here his broad brushstrokes convey the rippled reflections in the water.

A boat race is about to start.

Sunlight and snow.

The Magpie 1868–69

Monet painted a magpie perched on a gate, in order to add interest to this snowy country scene. The bold black and white bird helps lead our eyes into the background of the picture.

The Beach at Trouville 1870

Monet's wife, Camille, and her friend are sitting on the beach, shaded by parasols. Grains of sand stuck to the paint show that Monet painted the picture at the seaside, not in a studio.

Claude Monet's wife, Camille

La Grenouillère 1869

La Grenouillère was a floating café on the River Seine. People went there to swim and to hire rowboats. Monet and his friend the artist Auguste Renoir sat side by side to paint their own versions of this busy scene.

We are surrounded by water.

The Luncheon 1866 (central section)

Camille and some friends are enjoying a picnic. The dresses the women are wearing were the height of fashion at the time.

Women in the Garden 1866–67

Camille was the model for all four women here. Monet took great care painting the different patterns of each of the dresses.

I'm sitting on a riverbank.

On the Seine at Bennecourt 1868

In this peaceful scene Monet captures the effect of bright sunlight and deep shadows on the River Seine. He was very poor when he painted this, one of his earlier works.

Family life

Monet and his first wife, Camille, had two sons. The family shared a house at Vétheuil, near Paris, with Alice Hoschedé, her husband and their six children. After Camille died, the two families moved to Giverny, where, after the death of her husband, Alice and Claude were remarried to each other. Monet painted some of his most famous works in Giverny, and after suffering poverty for years, gained widespread acceptance and success.

The Terrace at Sainte-Adresse 1867

Monet painted this picture at the seaside in northern France. The man in the straw hat is his father. You can tell it's a windy day by looking at the flags and at the smoke from the ships' funnels.

The umbrella helps shade us from the sun.

Woman with a Parasol - Mme Monet and her Son 1875

Monet chose pale colors and dark shadows to show that it's a sunny day. The sketchy brushstrokes on Camille's dress create a feeling of movement. With her is her son Jean.

Wild Poppies 1873

Monet painted Camille and Jean on a sunny day among bright poppies. The contrast of red flowers and green background makes both colors appear especially bright.

May I pick the bright red flowers?

Monet and his family, under the lime trees at Giverny

The Luncheon 1868 (detail)

Camille is waiting for Monet to stop painting and take his place at the empty chair. Jean is bathed in the sunlight streaming through the window.

Boat at Giverny 1887

Three of Alice's daughters were the models in this
fishing scene. Monet was fascinated by their reflections
in the river. The vivid pinks and whites of the girls' dresses
contrast with the dark blues and greens of the water.

The Studio Boat 1874

In order to get close to the river, with its ever-
changing light and shade, Monet converted a
small boat into a floating studio. The boat had an
awning so that he could paint in all weathers.

Let's eat in
the garden.

The Luncheon 1873

Monet has painted a happy picture
of family life. Food is set out for
lunch in the shade of a tree.
Meanwhile the artist's son,
Jean, plays on the ground.

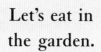

The Artist's Garden at Vétheuil 1880

This is the garden of the house where Monet
and his family lived at Vétheuil. The colorful
sunflowers towering over the children make
the picture particularly cheerful.

Coast and countryside

As well as painting near his home at Giverny, Monet went on excursions to the coast of northern France and to the Mediterranean Sea. He often worked on several pictures at once, switching from canvas to canvas as he tried to show how colors in the open air are affected by changes in the light and weather.

Grainstacks (End of Summer) 1891

Monet did twenty-five paintings of grainstacks, working for a few minutes at a time on each. His step-daughter Blanche would quickly slide each canvas onto the easel as he tried to capture the rapidly altering light.

Postcard of grainstacks near Giverny

These rocks are all wet.

Grainstack 1891

When people saw the grainstack paintings they loved their color and light, and the way Monet used them to show the various seasons.

This grainstack looks like an igloo.

Rocks at Belle Isle 1886

Monet worked beside the sea, dressed in fishermen's clothes, his easel held down with ropes and stones. Sometimes the gusts of wind were so strong they ripped the brushes and palette out of his hands.

The Customs House at Varengeville 1897

Cottages like this once belonged to customs men. When Monet painted this cottage, it was used by fishermen. He had to scramble around dangerous cliffs to reach the spot he painted from.

1

2

3

4

Do you know where
to put each sticker?
If you're not sure, you
can turn to page 12 and
check the sticker
numbers against the
answer key.

5

6

7

8

9

10

11

12

13

14

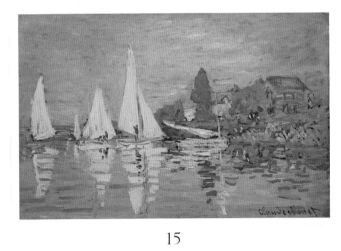

15

16

17

18

19

20

In the woods at Giverny - Blanche Hoschedé-Monet at her easel with Suzanne Hoschedé reading 1887

Blanche paints, while her sister Suzanne reads. Blanche, a talented artist, went on painting trips with Monet and carried his paints and easel for him.

Cliff Walk at Pourville 1882

Monet's paintings of the northern French coast were very popular. In this picture the small scale of the figures gives us a clue as to the height of the cliffs.

Keep away from the edge!

Poplars 1891

Near Monet's house was a line of poplar trees at the edge of the river. Monet fitted his canvases into slots inside a flat-bottomed boat and worked on three or four pictures at a time. He painted twenty-four versions of the trees in all.

These tall trees seem to touch the sky.

Poplars 1891

Monet painted this view from the boat on the river. From where he sat, he couldn't see the tops of the trees — which is why they appear to be cut off in the picture.

In the city

Although nature was Monet's first love, he returned to the city many times throughout his long life to paint buildings and busy streets. He visited London and Venice, where he painted the effect of the fog swirling around the grand buildings. At Rouen, near Paris, he painted thirty pictures of the front of the cathedral.

Waterloo Bridge (Cloudy day) 1899–1900

"What I like most about London," Monet said, "is the fog." But he became angry when the rain stopped him from painting!

Not a good day for sailing.

The Jetty at Le Havre 1867–70

The dark figures on the jetty stand out against the silver-gray sea. Monet painted the rough waves so realistically that we almost feel them breaking against the ships.

The Houses of Parliament, the Effect of Sun through the Fog 1904

On his first trip to London, Monet was fascinated by the River Thames and the reflection of the Houses of Parliament in the water. The soothing colors make this foggy scene very restful.

Monet and Alice in Venice

The Grand Canal, Venice 1908

On his trip to Venice, Monet was delighted by the beautiful palaces beside the canals. Here he contrasted the vertical lines of the mooring poles with the horizontal reflections.

Rue Montorgueil, Festival of 30 June 1878

Monet sat at a window high above the street to paint this buoyant view of Paris. He used dashes and blobs of paint to make the flags flutter.

It's a celebration!

Arriving at the station.

Arrival of the Normandy Train, Saint Lazare Station 1877

Monet loved to paint the effect of light on steam trains. He painted at least ten versions of trains at this station.

Cathedral at Rouen (Harmony in blue and gold, full sunlight) 1894

Monet sat inside a dress shop opposite the Rouen cathedral and painted thirty versions of this building. He applied the paint in thick layers to show the rough texture of the stone.

A dazzling religious building.

Rouen Cathedral Façade 1894

Monet worked on several canvases at once. He rushed from one to another trying to capture the changing light and colors on the front of the cathedral.

The garden at Giverny

Monet was passionate about gardening. He filled his garden at Giverny with beautiful flowers. He bought a piece of swampy land beyond the garden and made it into a pond in which he grew exotic water lilies. Monet spent much of the last thirty years of his life painting his water garden.

Monet's Garden at Giverny 1895
Here Monet used warm reds, oranges, and yellows for the roses, and cool green for the leaves.

These flowers would make a beautiful bouquet.

The Garden at Giverny 1900
Monet was very proud of his garden. He planned it so that there were colorful flowers to paint and admire all year round. Can you see Monet's house in this picture?

Monet admiring his flower garden

Japanese Bridge at Giverny 1900

A Japanese-style bridge arches over the lily pond in Monet's garden. Dark and mysterious reflections are balanced by bright yellow and green bushes.

Now we can walk over the water.

Spring 1886
Two girls relax under delicately painted plum trees in blossom. The bright colors allow us to feel this fresh spring day.

Water Lilies: Morning
1917–26 (left panel)

The bright lily pads on the left side of the painting contrast with the darkness of the pond.

Water Lilies: The Clouds
1917–26 (central panel)

Monet painted the reflections of the sky and clouds in the pond. His team of six gardeners kept the water very clean so that the reflections would be crystal-clear.

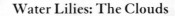

Is it sky or is it water?

Yellow and Mauve Irises 1924–25

Monet's favorite flower was the iris, whose slender green stems and bright purple, blue and yellow blossoms he often depicted. He planted clumps of irises around the edge of his pond.

Here's a picture of me!

Self-Portrait 1917

Many other artists painted Monet, but he rarely painted pictures of himself. By the time he did this self-portrait at seventy-seven, his eyesight was failing; still, he managed to paint some of his greatest works in his later years.

ABOUT THE AUTHOR

CAROLE ARMSTRONG has for many years been an art teacher and museum educator, working both in England and in the United States. At the Bayly Art Museum, University of Virginia, she introduced art activities, tours, workshops, poetry and art competitions for children. Among her other books are *All My Own Work!* (1993) and *My Art Museum* (1994).

THIS BOOK IS DEDICATED TO MURIEL & CHARLES

PHOTOGRAPHY ACKNOWLEDGMENTS

Key: *A* = above   *B* = below   *C* = center   *L* = left   *R* = right

The publishers have made every effort to contact all holders of copyright on the works reproduced in this book. All copyright holders who have not been reached are invited to contact the publishers so that full acknowledgment may be given in subsequent editions.

Images supplied by The Art Institute of Chicago copyright © 1995 The Art Institute of Chicago - All Rights Reserved.

Cover: Illustrations by Sarah Godwin; *L* © 1994 National Gallery of Art, Washington (collection of Mr. and Mrs. Paul Mellon); *R* The Art Institute of Chicago (Restricted gift of the Searle Family Trust; Major Aquisitions Centennial Endowment; through prior aquisitions of the Mr. and Mrs. Martin A. Ryerson and Potter Palmer Collections; through prior bequest of Jerome Friedman, 1983.29)

p. 1: Musée d'Orsay, Paris
Photograph: Philippe Piguet Collection

PAINTING OUT OF DOORS
p. 2: *A* Musée Marmottan/Bridgeman Art Library; *C, B* Musée d'Orsay, Paris
Photograph: Jean-Marie Toulgouat Collection

p. 3: *AL* The National Gallery, London; *CL* © 1989 The Metropolitan Museum of Art (Bequest of Mrs. H.O. Havemeyer, 1929. H.O. Havemeyer Collection, 29.100.112); *CR, BL* Musée d'Orsay, Paris; *BR* The Art Institute of Chicago (Potter Palmer Collection, 1922.427)
Photograph: A. Greiner, Amsterdam 1871, Private Collection

FAMILY LIFE
p. 4: *AL* ©1989 The Metropolitan Museum of Art, Purchased with special contributions and purchase funds given or bequeathed by friends of the Museum, 1967. (67.241); *AR* © 1994 National Gallery of Art, Washington (Collection of Mr. and Mrs. Paul Mellon); *CL* Musée d'Orsay, Paris; *BR* (detail) Städelsches Kunstinstitut, Frankfurt/Bridgeman Art Library
Photograph: Philippe Piguet Collection

p. 5: *AL* Musée d'Orsay/Giraudon/Bridgeman Art Library; *AR* Kröller-Müller State Museum, Otterlo, The Netherlands; *CR* Musée d'Orsay, Paris; *BL* National Gallery of Art, Washington/Giraudon/Bridgeman Art Library
Photograph: Philippe Piguet Collection

COAST AND COUNTRYSIDE
p. 6: *AL* The Art Institute of Chicago (Arthur M. Wood in memory of Pauline Palmer Wood, 1985.1103); *CL* The Art Institute of Chicago (Gift of Mr. and Mrs. Chauncey B. Borland, 1964.210); *CR* See acknowledgments for cover *R*; *BR* The Art Institute of Chicago (Mr. and Mrs. Martin A. Ryerson Collection, 1933.1149)
Photograph: Philippe Piguet Collection

p. 7: *AL* Los Angeles County Museum of Art (Mr. and Mrs. George Gard de Sylva Collection); *AR* The Art Institute of Chicago (Mr. and Mrs. Lewis Larned Coburn Memorial Collection, 1933.443); *CL* Fitzwilliam Museum, Cambridge/Bridgeman Art Library; *BL* ©1984 The Metropolitan Museum of Art (Bequest of Mrs. H. O. Havemeyer, 1929. H.O. Havemeyer Collection, 29.100.110)
Photograph: Rights reserved - Document Archives Durand-Ruel

IN THE CITY
p. 8: *AR* Hugh Lane Municipal Gallery of Modern Art, Dublin/Bridgeman Art Library; *C* Christie's, London/Bridgeman Art Library; *B* Musée d'Orsay/Giraudon/Bridgeman Art Library
Photograph: Rights reserved - Document Archives Durand-Ruel

p. 9: *AR* Museum of Fine Arts, Boston (Bequest of Alexander Cochrane); *CL* Musée d'Orsay/Lauros-Giraudon/Bridgeman Art Library; *CR* The Art Institute of Chicago (Mr. and Mrs. Martin A. Ryerson Collection, 1933.1158); *BL* Christie's, London/Bridgeman Art Library; *BR* Musée d'Orsay/Giraudon/Bridgeman Art Library
Photograph: Philippe Piguet Collection

THE GARDEN AT GIVERNY
p. 10: *AL* Musée d'Orsay, Paris; *AR* Foundation E.G. Bührle Collection; *BL* Fitzwilliam Museum, Cambridge/Bridgeman Art Library; *BR* The Art Institute of Chicago (Mr. and Mrs. Lewis Larned Coburn Memorial Collection, 1933.441)
Photograph: Rights reserved - Document Archives Durand-Ruel

p. 11: *AL, AR* Musée de l'Orangerie/Lauros-Giraudon/Bridgeman Art Library; *CR* Musée Marmottan; *B* Musée d'Orsay/R.M.N.
Photograph: Roger-Viollet

p. 12: Musée d'Orsay

p. 13: *Photograph: Philippe Piguet Collection*

STICKER KEY
Did you put each sticker in the correct frame?

1. Cliff Walk at Pourville **2.** La Grenouillère **3.** Rue Montorgueil, Festival of 30 June 1878
4. Arrival of the Normandy Train, Saint Lazare Station **5.** Grainstack **6.** Wild Poppies
7. Water Lilies: The Clouds **8.** Self-Portrait **9.** On the Seine at Bennecourt **10.** The Studio Boat
11. Monet's Garden at Giverny **12.** The Luncheon **13.** Cathedral at Rouen (Harmony in blue and gold, full sunlight)
14. The Jetty at Le Havre **15.** Regatta at Argenteuil **16.** The Magpie **17.** Rocks at Belle Isle **18.** Poplars
19. Woman with a Parasol—Mme Monet and her Son **20.** Japanese Bridge at Giverny